John Goodman

A Discourse Concerning Auricular Confession

as it is prescribed by the Council of Trent, and practised in the Church of

Rome

John Goodman

A Discourse Concerning Auricular Confession
as it is prescribed by the Council of Trent, and practised in the Church of Rome

ISBN/EAN: 9783337382087

Printed in Europe, USA, Canada, Australia, Japan

Cover: Foto ©Andreas Hilbeck / pixelio.de

More available books at **www.hansebooks.com**

A

DISCOURSE

CONCERNING

𝕬uricular𝕮onfeſsion,

As it is preſcribed by the

COUNCIL

OF

TRENT,

And practiſed in the

CHURCH of *ROME*.

With a Poſt-ſcript on occaſion of a Book
lately printed in *France*, called

Hiſtoria Confeſſionis Auricularis.
By Dr. Goodman. ~~John~~

LONDON,

Printed by *H. Hills* Jun. for *Benj. Tooke* at the Sign
of the *Ship* in St. *Paul's* Church-yard ; and
Fincham Gardiner at the Sign of the
White-Horſe in *Ludgate-ſtreet.* 1648.

O F

Auricular Confeſſion.

THE Zealots of the Church of *Rome*, are wont to Glory of the ſingular advantages, in the Communion of that Church, eſpecially in reſpect of the greater means and helps of Spiritual comfort, which they pretend are to be had there, above and beyond what are to be found amongſt other Societies of Chriſtians. Which one thing, if it could be as ſubſtantially made out, as it is confidently aſſerted, could not fail to ſway very much with all Wiſe men, and would undoubtedly prevail with all devout perſons, (who were made acquainted with the ſecret) to go over to them. But if contrariwiſe it appear upon ſearch, that their pretenſions of this kind are falſe and groundleſs, and that the methods of Adminiſtring conſolation, which are peculiar to that Church, are as well unſafe and deceitful, as ſingular and unneceſſary : Then the ſame Prudence and Sincerity, will oblige a man to ſuſpect that Communion, inſtead of becoming a proſelyte to it, and to look upon the aforeſaid boaſtings as the effect either of deſigned impoſture, or at the leaſt of Ignorance and Deluſion.

Amongſt other things, that Church highly values it ſelf upon, the Sacrament of Penance (as they call it) and as deeply blames and condemns the Church of *England*, and other Reformed Churches, for their defect in, and neg-

lect

lect of ſo important and comfortable an Office. And under that ſpecious pretext, her Emiſſaries who are wont according to the phraſe of the Apoſtle, *to creep into houſes, and lead Captive ſilly Women,* &c. inſinuate themſelves into ſuch of the People as have more Zeal then knowledge, and now and then wheadle ſome of them over into their Society. To that purpoſe, they will not only harangue them with fine ſtories of the eaſe and benefit of it, as of an Ancient and uſeful Rite, but will alſo Preach to them the neceſſity of it, as of Divine Inſtitution, and that it is as important (in its kind) as Baptiſm or the Lords Supper. For that Confeſſion to a Prieſt, and his Abſolution thereupon obtained, is the only means appointed by God for the procuring of Pardon of all mortal ſins committed after Baptiſm.

Concil. Trid. ſeſſ. 14. c. 2.

As for Original ſin, or whatſoever actual tranſgreſſions may have been committed before Baptiſm, all thoſe they acknowledg to be waſhed away in that ſacred Laver. And for ſins of Infirmity or Venial ſins, theſe may be done away by ſeveral eaſy methods, by Contrition alone (ſay ſome,) nay, by Attrition alone (ſay others) by Habitual Grace ſays a third, &c. But for mortal ſins committed after a man is admitted into the Church by Baptiſm, for theſe there is no other door of Mercy, but the Prieſts Lips, nor hath God appointed, or will admit of any other way of Reconciliation then this, of Confeſſion to a Prieſt, and his Abſolution.

Vid. Becan. Tract. de Sacramentis in ſpecie.

This Sacrament of Penance therefore is called by them, *Secunda Tabula poſt naufragium,* the peculiar refuge of a lapſed Chriſtian the only Sanctuary of a guilty Conſcience, the ſole means of reſtoring ſuch a perſon to Peace of Conſcience, the Favour of God, and the hopes of Heaven. And withal, this method is

held

held to be fo Soveraign and Effectual a remedy, that it cures *toties, quoties* ; and whatever a mans miscarriages have been, and how often foever repeated, if he do but as often resort to it, he shall return as pure and clean as when he first came from the Font.

This ready and easie way (say they) hath God allowed men, of quitting all scores with himself, in the use of which they may have perfect peace in their Consciences, and may think of the day of Judgment without horror, having their Cafe decided beforehand by Gods Deputy the Priest, and their Pardon ready to produce, and plead at the Tribunal of Chrift.

What a mighty defect is it therefore in the Proteftant Churches, who wanting this Sacrament, want the principal miniftry of reconciliation? And who would not joyn himfelf to the Society of that Church, where this great Cafe is fo abundantly provided for? For if all this be true, he muft be extreamly fool-hardy and deferve to perifh, who will not be of that Communion from whence the way to Heaven is fo very eafie and obvious, no wonder therefore I fay, if not only the loofe and vicious are fond of this Communion where they may fin and confefs, and confefs and fin again without any great danger, but it would be ftrange if the more Virtuous and Prudent alfo, did not out of more caution think it became them to comply with his expedient. For as much as there is no man who underftands himfelf, but muft be confcious of having committed fins fince his Baptifm, and then for fear fome of them should prove to be of a mortal nature, it will be his fafeft courfe to betake himfelf to this refuge, and confequently he will eafily be drawn to that Church, where the only remedy of his difeafe is to be had.

But the beft of it is, thefe things are fo oner faid then
proved

proved, and more eaſily phanſied by ſilly People, then believed by thoſe of diſcretion. And therefore there may be no culpable defect in the reformed Churches, that they truſt not to this remedy in ſo great a Caſe. And as for the Church of *England* in particular, though ſhe hath no fondneſs for Mounte-bank Medicines, as obſerving them to be ſeldom ſucceſsful; yet ſhe is not wanting in her care, and com-paſſion to the Souls of thoſe under her guidance, but ex-preſſeth as much tenderneſs of their peace and com-fort, as the Church of *Rome* can pretend to. Indeed ſhe hath not ſet up a Confeſſors Chair in every Pariſh, nor much leſs placed the Prieſt in the Seat of God Al-mighty, as thinking it ſafer, at leaſt in ordinary Caſes, to remit men to the Text of the written word of God, and to the publick Miniſtry thereof, for reſolution of Conſcience, then to the ſecret Oracle of a Prieſt in a corner, and adviſes them rather to obſerve what God himſelf declares of the nature and guilt of ſin, the ag-gravations or abatements of it, and the terms and conditions of Pardon, then what a Prieſt pronounces. But however this courſe doth not pleaſe the Church of *Rome*, for reaſons beſt known to themſelves, which if we may gueſs at, the main ſeems to be this, they do not think it fit to let men be their own carvers, but lead them like Children by the hand ; my meaning is, they keep People as much in Ignorance of the Holy Scripture as they can, locking that up from them in an unknown Tongue ; now if they may not be truſted with thoſe Sacred Records, ſo as to inform themſelves of the terms of the New Covenant, the conditions of the Pardon of ſin, and Salvation, it is then but reaſonable that the Prieſt ſhould Judge for them, and that they await their doom from his Mouth. Yet I do not ſee why in a Proteſtant Church,

where

where the whole Religion is in the Mother Tongue, the Old and efpecially the New Teftament conftantly, and confcientiously expounded, and the People allowed to fearch the Scriptures, and *to fee whether things be fo or no*, I fee not, I fay, Why in fuch a cafe the Prieft may not in great meafure be excufed the trouble of attending fecret Confeffions, without danger to the Souls of men.

But befides this, there is a conftant ufe of Confeffion and Abfolution too, in the Church of *England*, in every Days Service ; which though they be both in general terms, as they ought to be in publick Worfhip, yet every Penitent can both from his own Confcience fupply the generality of the Confeffion by a remorfeful reflection upon his own particular fins, as well as if he did it at the knees of a Prieft ; and alfo by an Act of Faith can apply the general Sentence of Abfolution to his own Soul, with as good and comfortable effects, as if it had been fpecially pronounced by his Confeffor.

But this publick Confeffion doth not pleafe the *Romanifts* neither, and they know a Reafon for their diflike ; namely, becaufe this doth not conciliate fo great a Veneration to the Prieft-hood, as when all men are brought to kneel to them for Salvation : Neither doth this way make them to pry into the fecret thoughts of Men, as Auricular Confeffion doth, wherein the Prieft is not only made a Judge of mens eftate, but a Spy upon their behavior, and is capable of becoming an Intelligencer to his Superiors of all the Defigns, Interefts, and even Conftitutions of the People.

Moreover the Church of *England* allows of private Confeffions alfo, as particularly in the Vifitation of the fick, (which office extends alfo to them that are troubled in Mind or Confcience, as well as to the afflicted in Body) where the Minifter is directed to examine

par-

particularly the ftate of the Decumbents Soul, to fearch and romage his Confcience , to try his Faith, his Repentance, his Charity, nay, to move him to make a fpecial Confeffion of his fins, and afterwards to abfolve him upon juft grounds.

Nay further yet, if (befides the cafe of Sicknefs) any Man fhall either out of perplexity of Mind, fcrupulofity or remorfe of Confcience, or any other devout confideration, think it needful to apply himfelf to a Prieft of the Church of *England* for advice, eafe, or relief, he hath incouragement and direction fo to do in the firft Exhortation to the Holy Communion, and may be fure to find thofe who will tenderly, and faithfully, as well as fecretly adminifter to his neceffities. So that I fee not what defect or omiffion can be objected to this Church in all this Affair, or what Temptation any Man can have upon this account to go from us to the Church of *Rome.*

But all this will not fatisfy them of the Church of *Rome,* they are neither contented with publick confeffion, nor with private, no nor with fecret neither, if it be only occafional or voluntary : It is the univerfality and neceffity of it which they infift upon, for it is not with them a Matter of Ecclefiaftical Difcipline, to prevent the Scandal of the Society, to conferve the Reverence of the Church, or to reftrain men from finning, or much lefs an Office of Expediency and Prudence to be reforted to upon exigencies, or fuch as may accidentally become neceffary upon emergency as fuppofe upon the atrocity of fome fact committed, the fcandaloufnefs of fome perfons former life, which may make him more doubtful of his Pardon, the weaknefs of his Judgment, the Melancholy of his Temper, or the Anxiety of his Mind, or any fuch like occafion, but it muft be the ftanding indifpenfable duty of all men,

men, as the condition of the Pardon of their Sins; in one word it muſt be a Sacrament of Divine inſtitution, and of Univerſal Obligation.

For ſo the Council of *Trent* determins, *Seſſ. 4 Canon* 1. *Si quis dixerit in Eccleſiâ Catholica pœnitentiam non eſſe verè & propriè Sacramentum pro fidelibus, quoties poſt Baptiſmum in peccata labentur, ipſi Deo reconciliandis a Domino noſtro inſtitutum, Anathema ſit;* i.e. Let him be accurſed, who ſhall affirm that Penance is not truly and properly a Sacrament inſtituted and appointed in the Univerſal Church, by our Lord Chriſt himſelf, for the reconciling thoſe Chriſt.ans to the Divine Majeſty, who have fallen into Sin after their Baptiſm.

And in the Doctrinal part of that Decree they teach and aſſert more particularly; Firſt, That our Saviour inſtituted this Sacrament expreſly, *Joh.* 20. 22.

2. That this Sacrament conſiſts of two parts, *viz.* Seſſ. 14. Cap. 2. the Matter and the Form; the Matter of the Sacrament (or *quaſi materia* as they cautiouſly ſpeak) is the act or acts of the Penitent, namely, Contrition, Confeſſion, and Satisfaction; the Form of it is the act of the Prieſt in theſe words, *Abſolvo te.*

3. That therefore it is the duty of every Man who Cap. 3. hath fallen after Baptiſm, as aforeſaid, to confeſs his ſins at leaſt once a year to a Prieſt.

4. That this confeſſion is to be ſecret; for publick Con- Cap. 5. feſſion they ſay is neither commanded nor expedient.

5. That this confeſſion of Mortal ſin be very exact and Ibid. particular, together with all circumſtances, eſpecially ſuch as *ſpeciem facti mutant*, alter the kind or degree of ſin, and that it extend to the moſt ſecret ſins, even of Ibid. thought, or againſt the 9th. and 10th. Commandment.

6. That the Penitent thus doing, the Abſolution of Cap. 6. the Prieſt hereupon pronounced is not conditional or declarative only, but abſolute and judicial. Now

Now in oppofition to this Doctrine and Decree of theirs, and the practice of that Church purfuant thereof, as well as in defence of the Doctrine and Practice of the Church of *England* in that particular, I will here endeavor to make good thefe Three things.

1. That our bleffed Lord and Saviour hath neither in his Gofpel inftituted fuch an Auricular Confeffion as aforefaid, nor much lefs, fuch a Sacrament of Penance as the Church of *Rome* fuppofes in the recited Decree.

2. That Auricular Confeffion hath not been of conftant and univerfal ufe in the Chriftian Church, as the *Romanifts* pretend, much lefs looked upon as of Sacramental and neceffary Obligation.

3. That Auricular Confeffion as it is now ufed in the Church of *Rome*, is not only unneceffary and burdenfome, but in many refpects very mifchievous to Piety, and the great ends of Chriftian Religion.

If the firft of thefe appear to be true, then (at the worft) the want of fuch an Auricular Confeffion in the reformed Churches, can be but an irregularity, and no effential defect.

If the fecond of thefe affertions be made good, then it can be no defect at all in thofe Churches that ufe not fuch a Rite, but a novelty and impofition on their parts who fo ftrictly require it.

But if the third be true, it will be the corruption and great fault of the Church of *Rome* to perfevere in the injunction and practice of it, and the excellency and commendation of thofe Churches which exclude it.

I begin with the firft, that it doth not appear that our Saviour hath inftituted fuch an Auricular Confeffion, of fuch a Sacrament of Penance as the Church of *Rome* pretends and practifes.

I confefs it is a Negative which I here undertake to make

make good, which is accounted a difficult Province, but the Council of *Trent* hath relieved us in that particular by founding the Institution expresly upon that one paſſage of the Goſpel, *Joh.* 20. 22. So that we ſhall not need to examine the whole Body of Scripture to diſcover what footſteps of Divine Inſtitution may be found ᴂere or there, for the Council wholly inſiſts and relies upon that Text of St. *John,* and therefore if that fail them, the whole *Hypotheſis* falls to the ground.

Now for the clearing of this, let us lay the words before us; and they are theſe, *He breathed on them, and ſaid, Receive ye the Holy Ghoſt, whoſoever ſins ye remit they are remitted unto them, and whoſoever ſins ye retain, they are retained.*

Now here I appeal to any Man that hath Eyes in his Head, or Ears to hear, whether i■ this Text there be any one word of Auricular Confeſſion, or much leſs of ſuch a circumſtantiated one as they require; And this is ſo manifeſt and notorious, that their own ancient Canoniſts, and ſeveral of their learned Divines are aſhamed of the pretence of Divine Inſtitution founded upon this or any other paſſage of Scripture, and therefore are content to defend the practice of the Church of *Rome* in this particular, upon the account of the Authority, and general uſage of the Church; which we ſhall come to examine by and by in its due place.

In the mean time I cannot chooſe but admire the mighty Faith of a *Romaniſt,* who can believe in ſpight of his own Eyes. It ſeemed to us an unſuperable difficulty heretofore, for a Man to perſuade himſelf that in the Sacrament of the Euchariſt Bread was tranſubſtantiated into Fleſh, becauſe it was againſt the expreſs Teſtimony of Senſe, yea, although for that there was

C   the

the countenance of Five figurative (but miſtaken)
words to ſupport the credulity ; but this of the Sacrament of Penance clearly out-does it, for here a Man
muſt believe a thing to be, when as there is not ſo much
as one word for the ground of his Faith, or the proof
of the thing in queſtion. How many Sacraments may
not ſuch men have if they pleaſe ? What voluminous
Creeds may not they ſwallow and digeſt ? What
Mountains may not ſuch a wonderful Faith remove?

But let us hear what they have to ſay for themſelves ;
perhaps in the firſt place they will plead the Authority
of the Council of *Trent*, which hath peremptorily de-
termined the ſenſe of the paſſage of the Goſpel to the
purpoſe aforeſaid. Indeed that Council in the third
Canon of their fourteenth Seſſion, doth damn all thoſe
who deny that a Sacrament of Penance and Auricular
Confeſſion is preſcribed in that Text of St. *John*, or
who apply it to any other purpoſe. But in ſo doing,
they both uſurp a Prerogative which was never pretended to or practiſed by any Council before them, and
withal they betray a conſciouſneſs that the Text it
ſelf yielded no ſufficient evidence of the thing which
they deſigned to countenance by it; for what Councils
(ever till now) brought a Text, and then impoſed an
Interpretation upon it contrary to the words? And then
backt that Interpretation with an *Anathema*? If the
Text were plain or could be made ſo, why was not
that done? And to be ſure if that cannot be done by
other means, the curſe will not do it ; at leaſt to any
but very obedient *Roman* Conſciences. Beſides if this
courſe be allowed, I ſee not but a Council may bring
in what Religion they pleaſe, having firſt made a Noſe
of Wax of the Holy Scripture, and then writhed it
into what ſhape they beſt phanſy ; for in ſuch a caſe, if
the words of the Goſpel do not favour me, I can go-
vern

vern the fenfe, and if the letter be filent or intractable, I can help that with an Interpretation ; and if I have authority or confidence enough to impofe that, under the peril of *Anathema*, I am no longer an Interpreter or a Judg, but a Law-giver, and need not trouble my felf with *Scriptum eft*, but may (if I will fpeak plain) fay *decretum eft*, and the bufinefs is done.

But if neither the Letter of Scripture, nor the Authority of a Council will do in this cafe, then in the fecond place they think they have at leaft fome colour of Reafon to relieve them ; and if they cannot find Auricular Confeffion in the Text, yet they will by confequence infer it thence ; for they fay although indeed it is true it is not here exprefly mentioned, yet it is certain that our Saviour in the Text before us inftituted a Sacrament of Penance, and therefore Auricular Confeffion muft neceffarily be implied becaufe abfolution cannot be without Confeffion.

Here the Reader will obferve that the point in Queftion between us is very much altered, for we are now fallen from the confideration of the Divine Inftitution of Auricular Confeffion in particular to that of a Sacrament of Penance in general, *i. e.* from a direct proof to a *fubintelligitur*. But we will follow them hither alfo, and for the clearing of this matter we will briefly confider thefe three things.

1. Whether that can properly be faid to be of Divine inftitution, and neceffary to Salvation, which depends on an inference, and is proved only by an *innuendo*?

2. Whether it can be reafonable to affert that our Saviour there inftitutes a Sacrament of Penance, where not only Auricular Confeffion, but the whole matter of fuch a Sacrament is left undefined ?

3. Whether if our Saviour (had done that which it is plain he hath not, that is,) had here inftituted and

appointed all thoſe things, which by the Church of
Rome are required as the material parts of Penance, yet
this could have been eſteemed a Sacrament?

1. For the firſt of theſe, we have no more to do but
to conſider the force and ſignification of this word *Inſtitution.* Now that in the common uſe of men (eſpecially of thoſe which ſpeak diſtinctly and underſtand-
ingly) implies a ſetting up *de novo*, or the appointing
that to become a duty, which was not knowable, or at
leaſt not known to be ſo before it became ſo appointed.
For this word *Inſtitution* is that which we uſe to expreſs
a poſitive command by, in oppoſition to that which is
Moral in the ſtricteſt ſenſe, and of natural obligation.
Now it is very evident that all things of this Nature
ought to be appointed very plainly and expreſly, or
elſe they can carry no obligation with them ; for ſee-
ing the whole Reaſon of their becoming matter of Law
or Duty, lies in the will of the Legiſlator, if that be
not plainly diſcovered, they cannot be ſaid to be inſtituted, and ſo there can be no Obligation to obſerve
them, becauſe *where there is no Law, there can be no Tranſ-
greſſion* ; and a Law is no Law in effect which is not
ſufficiently promulged. Is it not therefore a very
ſtrange thing to tell us of an Inſtitution by implication
only, and yet at the ſame time to tell us that the mat-
Seſſ. 14. C. 2. ter ſo (pretended to be) inſtituted, is no leſs then ab-
ſolutely neceſſary to the Salvation of Sinners?

2. The ſecond of theſe will eaſily be reſolved by con-
Seſſ. 14. C. 3. ſidering what we obſerved before from the Council of
Trent, *viz.* that this Sacrament of Penance conſiſts of
Matter and Form ; the Form is the Prieſts Abſolution,
but the Matter or Materials of this Sacrament are Contrition, Confeſſion to a Prieſt, and Satisfaction or Performance of the Penance enjoyn'd by him ; now it is evident
that not only Auricular Confeſſion (of which we have
                                                    ſpoken.

spoken hitherto but also Contrition and Satisfaction, are wholly omitted and past over in silence by the Evangelist in this passage of Scripture, from whence they fetch their Sacrament of Penance; and is it not a wonderfully strange thing, that our Saviour should be supposed to institute a Sacrament without any Materials of it at all? Surely therefore this must be either a very *Spiritual* Sacrament, or none at all.

Let us guess at the probability of this in proportion to either of the other undoubted Sacraments. Suppose our Saviour instead of that accurate form in which he instituted the Eucharist had only said, I would have you my Disciples and all that shall believe on my Name to keep a Memorial of me when I am gone : Or suppose he said only as he doth, *Joh. 6. 55. My Flesh is Meat indeed, and my Blood is drink indeed,* would any one have concluded here, that our Saviour in so saying, had appointed Bread and Wine to be consecrated, to be received in such a manner, and in a word that he had (without more ado) instituted such a Sacrament as we usually celebrate? No certainly, and therefore we see our Saviour is the most express and particular therein that can be, *for he takes Bread, blesses it, breaks it, gives it to them, saying, Take eat, this is my body,* &c. and *after Supper he takes the Cup, blesses it, gives it to them, saying, Drink ye all of this, for this is the New Testament in my Blood,* &c. and then adds, *do this in remembrance of me.* Now who is there that observes this accuracy of our Saviour in the Eucharist, can imagine that he should intend to institute a Sacrament of Penance, and that as necessary to Salvation (in the Opinion of the *Romanists*) as the other, only with this Form of words, *Whosoever sins ye remit they are remitted,* &c. and without the least mention of Confession, Contrition, or any other Material or necessary Part or Circumstance of it. 3. But

3. But in the third and last place, let us suppose that our Saviour had in the Text before us instituted Penance, and had appointed particularly all those things, which they call the Material parts of it, (as it is evident he hath not) yet even then, and upon that Supposition, Penance would not have proved to be a Sacrament properly so called.

I confess according to a loose acceptation of the word Sacrament, something may be said for it; for so there are many things have had the name of Sacrament applied to them. *Tertullian* somewhere calls *Elisha's* Ax the Sacrament of Wood, and in his Book against *Marcion* he stiles the whole Christian Religion a Sacrament. St. *Austin* in several places calls Bread, Fish, the Rock, and the Mystery of Number, Sacraments, for he hath given us a general Rule in his Fifth Epistle, *viz.* That all signs when they belong to divine things are called Sacraments : And in consideration hereof it is acknowledged by *Cassander*, that the Number of Sacraments was indefinite in the Church of *Rome* it self, until the times of *Peter Lombard.* But all this notwithstanding, and properly speaking, this Rite of Penance taking it altogether (and even supposing whatsoever the *Romanists* can suppose to belong to it)cannot be reputed a Sacrament, according to the allowed definitions of a Sacrament delivered by their own Divines. Some of them define a Sacrament thus, *a Sacramentum est corporale elementum foris sensibiliter propositum, ex similitudine repræsentans & ex institutione significans, & ex Sanctificatione continens invisibilem gratiam.* And the *b* Master of the Sentences himself describes it somewhat more briefly, but to the same effect in these words : *Sacramentum est invisibilis gratiæ visibilis forma, ejusdem gratiæ imaginem gerens & causa existens* ; both which definitions are acknowledged and applauded by the Jesuite *c Becanus* : And

a Hugo *de S.* Vict. *lib. de Sacram.*

b Magist. Sent. *lib. 4. dist. 1.*

c Becanus *Tract. 2. de Sacramentis.*

And the plain truth is a Sacrament cannot be better expreft in fo few words, then it is by St. *Auftin* when he calls it *verbum vifibile* a vifible Word or Gofpel : *Lib. 19. C. 16.* For it pleafed the Divine Wifdom and Goodnefs by this inftitution of Sacraments to condefcend to our weaknefs, and thereby to give us fenfible Tokens or Pledges of what he had promifed in his Written word, to the intent that our dulnefs might be relieved, and our Faith affifted ; forafmuch as herein, our Eyes and other Senfes as well as our Ears are made Witnefies of his gracious intentions. Thus by Baptifmal wafhing he gives us a fenfible token and reprefentation of our regeneration, and the wafhing away of our fins by the Blood of Chrift ; and by the participation of Bread and Wine in the Lords Supper we have a Token and Symbol of our Union with Chrift, our Friendfhip with God and Communion with each other.

But now it is manifeft there is no fuch thing as this in their Sacrament of Penance (as even *Bellarmine* himfelf confeffes.) For they do not fay or mean that the Abfolution of the Prieft is a Token or Emblem of God's forgivenefs, but that the Prieft actually pardons in God's ftead, by Virtue of a Power delegated to him. So that according to them, here muft be a Sacrament, not only without any material parts inftituted, but alfo without any thing Figurative, Symbolical or Significative, which feems to be as exprefly contrary to their own Doctrine in the aforefaid definitions, as to the truth it felf.

Nay, further to evince the difference of this Rite of Penance from all other proper Sacraments ; it deferves obfervation, that whereas in thofe other acknowledged Sacraments, the Prieft in God's Name delivers to us the Pledges and Symbols of Divine Grace. Here in this of Penance we muft bring all the material Parts and Pledges our felves, and prefent them to God, or

to

Aug. c. Fauft.

to the Prieſt in his ſtead : My meaning is, that where"
as (for inſtance) in Baptiſm the Prieſt applies to us
the Symbol of Water, and in the Euchariſt delivers to
us the conſecrated Elements in token of the Divine
Grace, contrary-wiſe here in Penance we muſt on our
parts bring with us Contrition, Confeſſion, and Satisfaction too, in which reſpect we may be rather ſaid
to give Pledges to God, then he to us ; which is wide-
ly different from the Nature of other Sacraments, and
ſeems no leſs to be contrary to the Reaſon and Notion
of a Sacrament in general.

The Sum of what we have hitherto diſcourſed,
amounts to this; Firſt, That here is no Auricular Confeſſion inſtituted by our Saviour, *Joh.* 20. 22. as was
pretended. Secondly, Nor, any Sacrament of Penance in
which it can be included or implied ; no nor indeed
any Sacrament at all.

I confeſs I might have ſpared all the words I have
uſed in proving the latter, for ſo long as I have made
appear that private Confeſſion is not inſtituted, it was
not ſo very material to conſider whether Penance could
be a Sacrament or no ; but this I added to ſhew the im-
perious dictates of that Church, and their extrava-
gancy in impoſing the moſt Sacred Names upon their
own inventions, thereby to give them the greater veneration with the People.

And thus I would diſmiſs the firſt part of my undertaking, but yet the *Romaniſts* will not forego their pretenſions for Auricular Confeſſion ; for they will yet
urge, that whether or no we will call it a Sacrament
which our Saviour inſtitutes in the Text before us, it
is however certain here is a Power conferred on the
Apoſtles, and their Succeſſors, of remitting and retain-
ing ſins ; for by theſe words, *Whoſoever ſins ye remit
they are remitted,* &c. * Our Saviour hath made the

* *Chriſtus con-
ſtituit Sacer-
dotes ſui ipſius
Vicarios.* Seſſ.
14. *Præſides &
Judices* Ibid. 4.

Prieſt

Prieſt a judge of Mens conſciences and conditions; wherefore that he may not proceed blindly and indiſcriminately it is neceſſary that he know the merits of the Cauſe, and not only underſtand the matter of fact, but all the circumſtances which may aggravate or extenuate it, all which cannot be attained without the Confeſſion of the party, therefore Auricular Confeſſion is as neceſſarily implied in the Text, as Abſolution or Retention of ſins is expreſt in it. So they.

Sacerdos ſolvit peccata poteſtate quadam prætoria Bellar. lib. 1. de ſacram. c. 10. Chriſtus ratam habet ſententiam à Sacerdote latam. id. lib. 3. c. 2.

But I crave leave to demand in the firſt place, Is it certain that upon ſuch a Confeſſion as they require, the Prieſt (as ſuch) will be able to make a right judgment of a Mans caſe that addreſſes himſelf to him, eſpecially conſidering the intricacy of ſome Caſes, and the ignorance of ſome Prieſts; upon this account are thoſe memorable words of St. *Auſtin Confeſſ. lib.* 10. *c.* 3. *Quid mihi ergo eſt cum hominibus ut audiant Confeſſiones meas, quaſi ipſi ſanaturi ſint omnes languores meos, & unde ſciunt cum à meipſo de meipſo audiunt, an verum dicam? Quando quidem nemo ſcit hominum quid agitur in homine, niſi ſpiritus hominis qui in ipſo eſt.* i. e. 'To what purpoſe ſhould I Confeſs my ſins to Men who cannot heal my wounds? 'For how ſhall they (who know nothing of my heart 'but by my own Confeſſion) know whether I ſay 'true or no? For no one knows what is in Man, but 'the Spirit of Man that is in him. O yes, they will ſay *clave non errante,* that is to ſay, if he judge right, he judges right, and no more, and this is mighty comfort to a diſtreſſed conſcience.

Secondly, Though we grant our Saviour hath given the Prieſt Authority to Remit and Retain ſins, yet how doth it appear that this extends to Secret ſins; ſins in thought only, or as the Council expreſſes it

againſt

against the ninth and tenth Commandments? Of open sins and publick scandals the Church hath cognizance, and hath a right which she may insist upon, or recede from, if she see cause, because such sins are an injury to the Society as well as an offence against God, and therefore here the Officers of the Church may dispense her Authority, and Remit or Retain (as we shall see more by and by;) but in secret sins where only God is injured, and to which he is only privy, what hath the Church to do, unless they be voluntarily discovered to her? Otherwise they are properly reserved Cases to the Tribunal of God.

Thirdly, I would be bold to enquire further, why may not sins, especially such as we last named, be Remitted upon Confession to God, without Confession to the Priest also? And I the rather ask this for these two reasons, First I observe that this very Council of *Trent* saith, that until the times of our Saviour, and his Institution of this Sacrament, sins were remitted upon contrition only, and application to the mercies of God, without Auricular Confession. They cannot therefore now say, remission implies this Confession, for that cannot be said to be implied in the nature of a thing, when the thing it self can be had without it.

Sess. 14. c. 1.

They will answer that it is sufficient, that it is now made necessary by our Saviour. But I reply, Then that Institution which now makes it necessary, must be better proved then yet it hath been, or else Men will be very apt to hope they may now under the Gospel obtain Pardon (at least) upon as easie terms as it was to be had at before.

My Second reason of asking that Third Question is this; I observe that their own Schoolmen acknowledg sins to be remitted under the Gospel by the

Aquinas summ. part. 3. Q. 68.

                                                    Priest

Prieft without any Confeffion to Men, particularly
in the Adminiftration of Baptifm, by which it plainly appears, that Confeffion is not implied in the
nature of Remiffion, but one may be had without
the other, and then why may not a finner after
Baptifm, hope for Pardon upon his contrite and devout application to the Word and Sacraments, without this new device and pick-lock of Confcience, Auricular Confeffion.

But fo much for that.

Sect. 3. I proceed now to the fecond thing propoun-
ded, namely, to inquire hiftorically whether or no
Auricular, or fuch a fecret, and Sacramental Confeffion, as aforefaid, hath been of conftant and univerfal ufe in the Chriftian Church, as the *Romanifts* pretend, and as the Council of *Trent* afferts, *Seffi.* 14.
Chap. 5.

This inquiry is not into matter of Law or Divine
Right, as the former was, but of Fact only, yet never
the lefs it is of great moment upon a double account:

1. Becaufe this is the ground which the Old *Roman*
Canonifts wholly went upon, (as I noted before;) they
exploded all pretence of Divine Inftitution in the cafe, as
having more modefty (it feems) then to pretend fo
high upon no better evidence, or at leaft they contented
themfelves to prefcribe for it only upon the Authority
of conftant and univerfal practice; now if we fhew the
falfenefs, of this ground, as well as of the other, then will
their Hypothefis of Auricular Confeffion have no foot
to ftand upon.

2. Becaufe the Credit of what hath been already
faid under the former head, doth very much depend
upon this, and that Difcourfe will be confirmed or
impaired refpectively to what fhall be evidently made
out in this fecond point. Forafmuch as if on the one

D 2　　　　　　　fide

ſide it be made apparent that ſuch a Rite hath been of conſtant uſe in the Chriſtian Church, it will afford a great preſumption that it took its riſe at firſt from Divine Inſtitution, notwithſtanding all we have offered to the contrary. So on the other ſide, if the Evidence here anſwer not the Pretenſion, and no ſufficient footſteps of conſtant and univerſal practice appear: Then will all that which we have hitherto diſcourſed, be greatly ſtrengthened and confirmed ; becauſe it is by no means probable, that if there had been a Divine Law in the caſe, that ſuch a thing would have been generally neglected by the Chriſtian Church.

Now for the clearing of this, though I am here only upon the defenſive, and ſo bound to no more then to examine the proofs which the *Romaniſts* bring for their pretenſions, yet I will deal ingenuouſly, as ſeeking not to find Flaws, but to diſcover the Truth, and therefore give theſe inſtances as ſo many reaſons for the Negative.

In the firſt place I crave leave to premiſe this : If Auricular Conſeſſion were ſo great a Goſpel myſtery, ſo wonderfully efficacious a method of ſaving Souls, as to be typified in the Law (as the *Romaniſts* teach) as well as inſtituted in the Goſpel and practiſed by the whole Church, one might ſeem juſtly to wonder how it comes to paſs that there ſhould be no mention, nor appearance of it in the whole courſe of our Saviours. own Miniſtry; he uſed to be an example, as well as a Law-giver to the Church, he waſhed his Diſciples Feet, before he enjoined them to waſh one another; he exemplified the other Sacraments before he preſcribed his Apoſtles to adminiſter them, & one would have thought ſuch an Inſtance of his example had been more neceſſary in this buſineſs of Penance, rather than any other, if it
had

had been but to make way for the Underftanding of fo
obfcure an Inftitution ; fince efpecially, one would have
thought to find fome Traces of this in the Miniftry of
our Saviour, becaufe he daily converfed with finners, he
reproved them, inftructed them, healed them, pardoned
them, but never brought any of them to fuch a Confeffion as we are treating of ; *viz.* To a particular enu-
meration of their fins with the circumftances, nor upon fo doing formally abfolved them. His very Difciples
(fome of which had been great finners) were admitted without it ; the Woman of *Samaria* was told by
him all that ever fhe did, but fhe was not brought on her
knees to make her own Confeffion ; but moft ftrange
of all it is, that the Woman taken in Adultery, when he
had made her accufers flink away, was not privately
brought to it ; it may be they will fay, there was no
need of Confefsion to him who knew all before, but yet
it might have been neceffary to bring thefe Sinners to
be afhamed of themfelves by that means to work Repentance, and fit them for Pardon, at leaft if this Method had been of fuch mighty ufe and wonderful neceffity as is pretended.

2. But to let pafs that ; in the next place it is matter of wonder that nothing of this practice appears in
the Miniftry of the Apoftles ; they went about preach-
ing the Gofpel, calling Men to Repentance, erecting and governing Churches, but never fet themfelves down in a Confeffors Chair for penitents, fecretly to tell them in their Ear, the Story of their vicious
Lives ; indeed we read, *Acts* 19. 18. That fome came
in and fhewed their deeds ; but firft it was voluntary,
and in a fit of Holy Zeal, for we cannot find that they
were required to do it, as of SacramentalObligation ; &
befides, the Confeffion was publick before the Church,
not clancular, and whifpered in fecret ; it is true al-

so that St. *James, chap.* 5. 16. advises the Christians to confess their faults one to another, (which is made a mighty evidence in this Case;) but it is as true, that this was spoken in an extraordinary Case, as appears *v.* 14. in bodily sickness and distress of Conscience, they are advised to lay open their condition, in order to relief and succour, by the more ardent and affectionate Prayers of those who should be made privy to it, but it is not made a standing and universal rule for all Men to comply with, whether they be sick or well, in prosperity or adversity, perplexed or quiet in their Consciences, much less of Sacramental and Necessary Obligation, as in the *Roman* Church.

3. Let us go on in the next ages after the Apostles, for about two hundred years we find not one word of this kind of Confession, which we enquire for. Indeed the writings of that time which are extant, are not many, but if this business had been of such consequence as is pretended, it is strange that those Holy Men *Ignatius*, *Clemens* and *Justin* Martyr, should not have any mention of it.

Indeed *Bellarmine* brings us one instance within this Period, and that is from *Irenæus*, who speaking of Certain Women who had been abused by *Marcion* the Heretick, saith they afterwards came and Confessed all, with shame and sorrow, to the Church. But what is this to the purpose? We dispute not against publick Confession, which is acknowledged to be truly Primitive, and we wish it had been constantly maintained in after ages, it is only the necessity of Clancular Confession that we are unsatisfied in, and this passage speaks nothing at all to that Case.

4. In *Tertullians* time, which was also much about Two hundred Years after our Saviour, we find great things said of Confession, but it is of that which was publick, and in the face of the Church, not to a Priest in a Corner, and this indeed was greatly incouraged and required by the Holy Men of those times, as that which in the Case of open and scandalous sins, freed the Church both from the guilt, and from the reproach of them, and in the Case of secret sins, was a means (by open shame) to bring Men to Repentance, and so to Pardon. And the Confession was principally directed to God, who was the person offended by the sin, yet it was made before Men to raise a fervency in their Prayers, as is noted before, and to obtain their effectual intercession with God on behalf of the penitent. This that Ancient writer makes manifest to be his Sense in his Book *de Pœnitentia* in these words *Plerumque vero jejuniis preces alere, ingemiscere, lachrymari, & mugire dies noctésque ad Dominum Deum tuum, Presbyteris advolvi, & aris* (or rather *charis*) *dei adgeniculari, omnibus fratribus legationes suæ deprecationis injungere, hæc omnia ex homologesis ut pænitentiam commendet, &c.* the penitent often joyns Fasting to his prayers, weeps, wails and moans night and day before God, casts himself at the feet of the Priests, kneels to all holy people, and intreats all the Brethren to be his Intercessors with God Almighty for his Pardon: This is penitential Confession, *&c.* And in his Apology more plainly ; *Coimus in Cœtum,* &c. *ibidem exhortationes, castigationes & censura divina nam & judicatur magno cum pondere ut apud certos de Dei conspectu, summumq; futuri judicii præjudicium est si quis ita deliquerit ut à communione,* &c. *religetur ;* we have (saith he) in our Ecclesiastical Assemblies, a Spiritual Judicature, and with great gravity,

Tertull. Apol. c. 39.

vity cenfure offenders, &c. But I need fay no more of
this; for we have the Teſtimony of *Beatus Rhenanus*,one

Beatus Rhen. in. in praef. ad Tertull. de pae- itent. of the *Roman* Church and of great infight into Ecclefia-
ſtical Affairs, who gives us this account of *Tertullian*
and his times, *nihil illum de clancularia illa poenitentia
loqui, quae id temporis penitus ignorabatur;* there was no
ſuch thing as ſecret or Clancular Confeſsion in-uſe in
Tertullian's time, which was a thing not fo much as
known by the Chriſtian Church in thofe days.

5. To go a little lower, ſuch was the manner of
proceedings in St. *Cyprian*'s time, as he himſelf defcribes

St. Cyprian. Lib. 3. Eph. 15. it, the finner by outward geftures and tokens fhew'd
himſelf to be ſorrowful and penitent for his fin, and
then made humble Confeſsion thereof before the whole
Congregation, and defired all the Brethren to pray
for him; which done, the Biſhop and Clergy laid their
hands upon him, and fo reconciled him: So it was al-

Origen in Pf. 37. ſo in *Origen*'s time, and once for all, to deliver the Cuſtom of the Church in thofe times, touching this

Sozomen L. 7. Cap. 16. particular, I will add the words of the Hiſtorian, *Rei
ad terram ſe pronos abjiciunt,* &c. they that are Con-
ſcious to themſelves to have offended, fall down flat
upon the ground with Weeping and Lamentations in
the Church, on the other ſide the Biſhop runs to them
with tears in his Eyes, and falls down to the ground,
alfo in token of Sorrow and Compaſſion, and the
whole Congregation in the mean while Sympathizing
with both, is overwhelmed with tears, &c.

6. If we go lower yet to the times of St. *Chryfoſtom*

St. Chryfoſt. ad Hebr. Homil. 31. Id. in Serm. de Confeſſ. & Poe- nit. &c. and St. *Auſtin*, we find thofe Holy Men ſpeaking very
flightly of Confeſſions to Men, fo little did they think
of Auricular Confeſſion being a Sacrament. St. *Auſtin*'s Judgment in the cafe we have heard before, in
the Tenth Book of his Confeſſions, and third Chapter;
and for the other, the Teſtimonies out of him are fo
many

many, and ſo well known, that I cannot think it neceſſary to tranſcribe them ; and as for St. *Jerom* who
lived about the ſame time, I think it ſufficient to repeat
the account of *Eraſmus*, who was very converſant in
his Writings, and indeed of all the other Fathers, and
who had no other fault I know, but that he did uſe
Mordaci radere vero, to be too great a Tell-truth ;
which ſure will not invalidate his Teſtimony ; his
words are theſe, *Apparet tempore Hieronimi nondum
inſtitutam fuiſſe ſecretam admiſſorum Confeſſionem.——
Verùm in hoc labuntur Theologi quidam parum attenti,
quòd quæ veteres ſcribunt de publica & generali confeſſio-
ne,ea trahunt ad occultam & longè diverſi generis, i.e.* It
is evident (ſaith he) that in St. *Jerom's* time (which was
about Four hundred years after our Saviour) there was
no ſuch thing as Secret Confeſſion in uſe;but the miſtake
is that ſome few later and inconſiderate Divines have
taken the inſtances of general and publick Confeſſion
then practiſed, for arguments of that Auricular Confeſſion which is now uſed, though quite of a different
nature from it.

.Thus we have traced the Current of Antiquity for
Four or Five hundred years to ſearch for the Head of
this *Nilus*, the ſource and riſe of that kind of Confeſſion which is ſo highly magnified by the Church of
Rome, but hitherto we have found nothing of it, and
this methinks ſhould be ſufficient to ſtagger an impar-
tial inquirer, (at leaſt it is as much as can be expected in
ſo ſhort a Treatiſe as this is intended to be) and may
ſatisfy the unprejudicate, that there is as little of Antiquity to favour this Rite, as there is of Divine Inſtitution to be pleaded for it. But yet I know on the other
ſide, that the *Romaniſts* pretend to bring abundance
of Teſtimonies for it, and *Bellarmine* particularly goes
from Century to Century with his Citations to pre-

ſcribe

scribe for the conſtant and uninterrupted uſe of it, but I do ſincerely think that theſe Four following ſhort Obſervations will inable a Man to anſwer them all.

1. I obſerve that whereas this word *Exomologeſis* is commonly uſed by diverſe of the Fathers, as the Phraſe whereby they intend to expreſs the whole nature of Repentance in all the parts and branches of it, as is evident by the paſſage I cited out of *Tertullian de Pœnit.* even now, and is acknowledged by *Bellarmine* himſelf; nevertheleſs, merely becauſe that word ſignifies Confeſſion properly, and nothing elſe, theſe *Romiſh* Sophiſters, where they find this word *Exomologeſis*, force it into an Argument for that Confeſſion, which they contend for; and ſo ſeveral Diſcourſes of the Fathers, concerning Repentance in general, are made to be nothing but *Exhortations* to, or *Encomiums* of Confeſſion in particular, and that muſt be nothing elſe neither but Auricular Confeſsion, the thing in Queſtion. A caſt of his skill in this way, *Bellarmine* gives us in *Irenæus*, the very firſt Author he cites for Auricular Confeſsion in the laſt quoted Book and Chapter of his Writings *De Sacramentis.*

2. Whereas the Novatians excluded all hopes of Repentance or Pardon for ſins committed after Baptiſm, but the true Church contrariwiſe admitted to hopes of Pardon upon their Repentance; upon this occaſion, when ſome of the Fathers juſtly magnify the advantages, and comfortableneſs of the true Church above the Schiſmatical, as that it ſet open a Door of Hope to thoſe who confeſſed their ſins, and applied themſelves to her Miniſtry. : Hence theſe witty men will perſuade the World, that every true Church had a Confeſſors Chair, and ſuch a formal way of pardoning as they now practiſe at *Rome* ; as if there was no remiſsion,

miſſion of Sin, where there was no Auricular Confeſſion, and as if all that excluded the latter, rejected
the former too, and were no better than Novatian
Hereticks; whenas in Truth the Power of the Keys
is exerciſed in all the Miniſtries of the Church, and
ſhe Pardons and retains Sins, otherwiſe than by the
Oracle of a particular Confeſſor, as we have ſeen al- Bellarm.
ready. This piece of jugling the ſame *Bellarmine* is *de Pœnit.*
alſo guilty of in his Citation of *Lactantius.* *Lib.* 3. C. 8.

3. Whereas the Ancient Writers are much in the
Commendation of Confeſſion of Sins, whether it be
to God or to the Church, but generally intending
that which is Publick, it is common with thoſe of
the Church of *Rome*, to lay hold of all ſuch ſayings as
were intended to perſuade to, and incourage publick
Confeſſions, and to apply them to Auricular or Clan-
cular Confeſſions, thus particularly the aforeſaid Au- *Id. Lib.* 3. C. 6.
thor does by *Tertullian* in his Citation of him.

4. And Laſtly, Whereas it is alſo true that ſeveral of
thoſe Holy Men of Old, do in ſome caſes very much
recommend Confeſſion of ſecret ſins, and perſuade
ſome ſorts of Men to the uſe of it, namely thoſe that
are in great perplexity of Conſcience, and that needed
Ghoſtly Counſel and Advice, or to the intent that
they might obtain the aſſiſtance of the Churches
Prayers, and make them the more ardent and effectual on their behalf, whereas I ſay, they recommended
this as an expreſſion of Zeal, or a prudent expedient,
or at moſt as neceſſary only in ſome caſes *pro hic &*
nunc. Theſe great Patrons of Auricular Confeſſion do
with their uſual artifice apply all theſe paſſages, to
prove it to be a ſtanding and univerſally neceſſary
duty, a Law to all Chriſtians; this is a very common
fault amongſt them, and particularly St. *Cyprian* is
thus miſapplied by the ſame forementioned Writer,
Lib. 3 .*Cap.* 7. E 2 Hi-

Hitherto inquiring into the moſt Ancient and Pureſt times of the Church, by the Writings of the Fathers of thoſe times, we have not been able to diſcover any ſufficient ground for ſuch an Auricular Confeſsion, as the Church of *Rome* pretends to, much leſs for a conſtant and uninterrupted ſucceſsion of it. But now after all I muſt acknowledge there is a paſſage in Eccleſiaſtical Hiſtory which ſeems to promiſe us ſatisfaction herein, and therefore muſt by no means be ſlightly paſſed over without due conſideration; it is the famous ſtory of *Nectarius* Biſhop of *Conſtantinople*, and Predeceſſor to St. *Chryſoſtom*, which happen'd ſomething leſs then Four hundred years after our Saviour.

Socrat. *Hiſt.* Lib. 5. Cap. 19. Sozomen. *Lib.* 7. C. 16.

The Story as it is related by the joint Teſtimony of *Socrates* and *Sozomen* runs thus : In the time of this *Nectarius* there was (it ſeems) a Cuſtom in that Church (as alſo in moſt others) that one of the Presbyters of greateſt Piety, Wiſdom, and Gravity ſhould be choſen Penitentiary, that is, be appointed to the peculiar Office of receiving Confeſsions, and to aſſiſt, and direct the Penitents in the management of their Repentance : Now it happens that a certain Woman of Quality, ſtricken with remorſe of Conſcience, comes to the Penitentiary (that then was) and according to Cuſtom, makes a particular Confeſsion of all ſuch ſins, as ſhe was conſcious to her ſelf to have committed ſince her Baptiſm, for which he according to his Office appointed her the Penance of Faſting, and continual Prayers to expiate her Guilt, and give proof of the Truth of her Repentance. But ſhe proceeding on very particularly in her Confeſsions, at laſt amongſt other things comes to declare that a certain Deacon of that Church had lien with her ; upon notice of which horrid Fact, the Deacon is forthwith caſhier'd and caſt out of the Church : By which means the miſ-

car-

carriage takes Air, and coming to the knowledge of the People, they prefently fall into a mighty commotion and rage about it, partly in deteftation of fo foul an Action of the Deacon, but principally in contemplation of the Difhonour, and Scandal thereby reflected on the whole Church. The Bifhop finding the Honour of the whole Body of his Clergy extreamly concern'd in this accident, and being very anxious what to do in this cafe, at laft by the Counfel of one *Eudæmon* a Presbyter of that Church, he refolves thenceforth to abolifh the Office of Penitentiary, both to extinguifh the prefent flame, and to prevent the like occafion for the future; and now by this means every Man is left to the Conduct of his own Confcience, and permitted to partake of the Holy Myfteries at his own peril. This is the matter of fact faithfully rendered from the words of the Hiftorian; but this, if we take it in the grofs, and look no further then fo, will not do much towards the deciding of the prefent Controverfy, we will therefore examine things a little more narrowly by the help of fuch hints as thofe Writers afford us, perhaps we may make good ufe of it at laft; and to this purpofe,

1. I obferve in the firft place, that though at the firft blufh here feems to be an early and great example of that Auricular Confeffion which we oppofe, forafmuch as here is not only the Order of the Church of *Conftantinople*, for Confeffion to a Prieft, but that to be of all fins committed after Baptifm, and this to be made to him in fecret; notwithftanding upon a more thorough view it will appear quite another thing from that pleaded for, and practifed by the Church of *Rome*, and that efpecially in the refpects following : Firft, In the Auricular Confeffion in the Story, there is fome remainder of the ancient Difcipline of the Church
(whofe

(whofe Confeffions ufed to be open and publick, as I
have fhewed in that here a publick Officer is appointed
by the Church to receive them, fuch an one as whofe
Prudence, and Learning, and Piety fhe could confide
in for a bufinefs of fo great nicety and difficulty, and
it is neither left to the Penitent to choofe his Confident
for his Confeffor, nor at large for every Prieft to reprefent the Authority of the Church in fo ticklifh an
Affair as that of Difcipline, but to a publick Officer
appointed by the Church for this purpofe; fo that
Confeffion to him cannot be faid to be private, feeing
it is done to the whole Church by him. To confirm
which, *Secondly*, This Penitentiary it feems was
bound (as there was occafion) to difcover the matters
(opened to him in fecret) to the Church, as appears in
the Crime of the Deacon in the Story; there was no pretence of a Seal of Confeffion in this Cafe, as in the
Church of *Rome*, by Virtue of which a Man may confefs and go on to fin again fecretly, without danger of
being brought upon the Stage, whatfoever the atrocity of his Crime be, and indeed without any effectual
courfe in Order to his Repentance and Reformation.
Again, *Thirdly*, This Confeffion in the Story doth
not pretend to be of abfolute neceffity as if a Mans
fins might not be pardoned without it; but only a
prudent Provifion of the Church to help Men forward
in their Repentance, to direct the Acts and Expref-
fions of it, and efpecially to relieve perplexed and
weak Confciences, and to affift them in their prepara-
tions for the Sacrament of the Lord's Supper; and this
appears, amongft other things, by the account which
the Hiftorian gives us of the confequence of abolifhing
it, *viz.* That now every Man is left to his own Confcience
about his partaking of the holy Myfteries; but it is
not faid or intimated that he was left under the guilt of
his

his Sins, for want of Confeſſion. To which add in the
laſt place, that this Office whatever it was, was not
reputed a Sacrament, but rather, as I noted before,
an expedient to prepare men for it, for doubtleſs neither that Biſhop, nor that Church would have ever
conſented to the abolition of a Sacrament, for the ſake
of ſuch a Scandal as happen'd in the miſmanagement
of it, or if they had done ſo, much leſs can it be imagined that the greateſt part of the Chriſtian Church
would have concurred with them in it, as we ſhall by
and by ſee they did.

2. I obſerve concerning the beginning of this Penitentiary Office, the time and occaſion of this uſage;
namely, that the Hiſtorians do not pretend it to have
been Apoſtolical, much leſs of ſtrictly Divine Inſtitution, but they lay the Heat of its firſt riſe about the time
of the *Decian* Perſecution, which was about Two hun-
dred years after our Saviour. I confeſs *Nicephorus* would Nicephor.*Lib.*
12. *Cap.* 28.
perſuade us of its greater Antiquity, and that it was
rather revived then inſtituted at that time, for he
ſpeaking of the bringing it into uſe at the *Decian* Perſecution ſaith , ἐκκλησιαστικῷ κανόνι ἑπόμενῳ, *i. e.* the
Church purſuant of the Ancient Eccleſiaſtical Canons
conſtituted a Penitentiary, &c. And *Petavius* is ſo ad-
dicted to the *Roman* Hypotheſis, as very unreaſonably
to favour this Conceit; but the Truth ſeems to be (as
Valeſius very ingenuouſly acknowledges) only this,
that here was a miſtake of the import of the words of
the Hiſtorian, who ſaith only that when the Church
had choſen their Penitentiary κανόνι προσέθεσαν, they
added him to the Canon, that is to the number of
thoſe in the *Matricula* or Roll of ſuch as were to be
maintain'd in and by the Church, or as we would ſay
they made him Canon of the Church; not that he
was Conſtituted in ſuch an Office, purſuant of an An-
cienter

cienter Law or Canon, as *Nicephorus* carelesly or wil-
fully miftakes. Befides afterwards when the Hiftorian
obferves that the Novatians univerfally withftood this
Order from the beginning of it, he calls it προσθήκην
ταύτην; *q. d.* this new Inftitution, or Addition, or
Supplement of the Ancient Rites of the Church; fo
that there is no reafon we fhould date this Inftitution
higher then the Hiftorian doth, namely, after the
Decian Perfecution.

But what fhould be the ground and reafons of
erecting this new Office, and Officer in the
Church then, if it was not before? Of this I give two
accounts.

Firft, The Church being now very nume-
rous, and the Zeal and Devotion very great; and
what by the compaffionate reception which the
Church gave to Penitents, and her ardent Prayers for
them, what by the earneft harangues of Holy Men
to move People to repentance, abundance were inclined to confefs their fins, and this Confeffion being till
that time accuftomed to be open, and publick in the
face of the Congregation, it muft needs happen (all
thofe circumftances confidered together) that a great
many things would be brought npon the Stage, the
Publication of which would be attended with great inconveniences; for fome fins are of that Nature, that
they fcarce can take Air without fpreading a Con-
tagion, fome Confefsions would make fport for
light and vain Perfons, and befides abundance
of other inconveniences (eafy to be imagined by any
one) the publication of fome fins might expofe the
Penitents to the Severity of the Pagan Criminal Judge;
upon thefe and fuch like confiderations, the Church
thought fit therefore I (as have intimated before) to
appoint one wife and very grave Perfon in her ftead to
receive

receive the Confessions; who by his discretion might so discriminate matters, that what things were fit for silence, might have private Methods applied to them, but what were fit to be brought upon the Stage, might be made Publick examples of, or receive a Publick remedy.

Secondly, But the Historian leads us to a more special Reason of this Institution at that time; namely, that the rage of the *Decian* Persecution cruelly shook the Church, and abundance of her weaker members fell off in the Storm, and, which was worst of all, the Church was distracted about the restitution or final rejection of those that had so miscarried; for though the best and wisest of the Church were so merciful and considerate of humane infirmity, as to be willing to receive those in again, upon Repentance, over whom the Temptation of fear had too much prevailed, yet the Novatians a great and Zealous part of Christianity, looked upon such as desperate, who had once broken their baptismal Vow, and would rather separate from the Church themselves, than suffer such to be restored to it. Here the Church was in a great strait, either she must be very severe to some, or she shall seem very unkind to others, she must either let the weak perish, or she must offend them that counted themselves strong. Now in this case she being both tenderly compassionate towards those that had fallen, and withal willing to satisfie those Novatian Dissenters, or at least to deliver her self from Scandal, takes this course, she requires that those who had fallen, and desired to be restored again to her Society, should acknowledge their faults, and make all the Penitent satisfaction that was possible for them to perform, that so neither they may be too easily tempted to do so again by the gentleness of the remedy, nor the

F   No-

Novatians reproach her Lenity, or take pet, as if no difference was made between the found and the lapfed ; for thefe caufes, though the moft publick Penance was thought little enough to be undergone by the lapfed ; but yet on the other fide, confidering wifely the inconveniences of publick Penance in fome cafes (as I fpecified before) fhe therefore took this middle courfe ; namely, fhe appointed a publick Confeffor, who having firft heard privately the feveral cafes of the Penitents, fhould bring into publick, only fuch of them as (without incurring any of the aforefaid dangers) might be made exemplary. And this appears to be the true reafon of this Inftitution, and the bottom of this affair, by this remarkable paffage in the Hiftorian ; That whereas the generality of the Orthodox clofed prefently with this wife temperament, the Novatians only, thofe felf conceited Non-conformifts, rejected προσδήκην ταύτην, this expedient as a new invention ; they were too humourfome to comply with fuch a temperament.

But here another Queftion arifes , *viz.* How far this new expedient was imbraced by the Orthodox Churches, for if it was only received by that of *Conftantinople*, the Authority would not be fo great ; for it is poffible to imagine, that other Churches might allow every private Prieft to confefs, and fo admit of no publick Penitentiary.

To which I anfwer, that by the Hiftory it feems plain enough, that this was not the peculiar manner of the Church of *Conftantinople* only, but the ufual Method in that time of moft other Churches alfo ; but I muft needs fay, I do not find that the Church of *Rome* complied with them herein, though it was not much to her Honour to be fingular, where there was fo much Prudence and Piety to have inclined her to Uniformity.

formity.   However this is gained, which is my point, that the Church of *Rome* is not countenanced in her practice of private and clancular Confeſſions, by the general uſage of the Church, as they pretend.

3. I obſerve concerning this Office of Penitentiary, that as it was erected upon prudential conſiderations, ſo it was upon the ſame grounds aboliſhed, by the ſame Authority of the Church which firſt inſtituted it, and that after about Two hundred years continuance in the time of *Nectarius*, as we have ſeen ; & therein he was followed, ſaith *Sozomen* by almoſt all the Biſhops and Churches in the World ; this therefore was far from being thought either a Divine or Apoſtolical Conſtitution : *Petavius* would here perſuade us, that it was only publick Confeſſion, and not private, which was upon this occaſion ſo generally laid aſide, as we have ſeen, but this is done by him more out of tenderneſs of Auricular Confeſſion, than upon good reaſon ; and *Valeſius* goes beyond him, and will needs perſuade us, that neither publick nor private Confeſſion were put down in this juncture, but only that the lately erected Officer of Penitentiary was caſhier'd ; but I muſt crave leave to ſay, there is no ſufficient reaſon for either of theſe conjectures, but on the contrary plain Evidence againſt them, for *Socrates*, who is the firſt and principal relater of this whole ſtory ſaith he was perſonally acquainted with this Presbyter *Eudemon*, who gave the advice to *Nectarius* to make this change in the Diſcipline of the Church, and that he had the aforeſaid relation of it from his own Mouth, and expoſtulated with him about it, giving his reaſons to the contrary, and ſuggeſted his ſuſpicions that the ſtate of Piety would be much endamaged by this change, and in plain words tells him, that he had now bereft men of aſſiſtance in the conduct of their Conſciences, and

hundred

hindred the great benefit men have, or might have one of another by private advice and correption. Now this fear of his had been the abſurdeſt thing in the World, if upon this counſel and advice of his, only one certain Man in the Office of publick Confeſſioner had been laid aſide, but both the uſe of publick and private Con- feſſions had been kept up and retained.

But after all (for ought appears) the Church of *Rome* kept her old Mumpſimus, ſhe tenacious of her own cuſtoms eſpecially of ſuch as may advance her Intereſt and Authority, complies not with this Inno- vation or Reformation (be it for better or worſe) but her Prieſts go on with their Confeſſions, and turn all Religion almoſt into Clancular Tranſactions, in de- ſpight of the example of other Churches. It may be ſhe met with oppoſition ſometimes, but ſhe was for- ced to diſemble it till the Heroick Age of the School- men, and then thoſe luſty Champions with their Fu- ſtian-ſtuff of *videtur quod ſic,& probatur quod non*, make good all her pretenſions. After them in the year 1215 comes the Fourth *Lateran* Council, and that decrees Auricular Confeſſion to be made by every body once a year at the leaſt ; and laſt of all comes the Council of *Trent*, and declares it to be of Divine Inſtitution, ne- ceſſary to Salvation, and the conſtant and univerſal cuſtom of the Chriſtian Church: And ſo we have the Pedigree of the *Romiſh* Auricular Confeſſion.

*Sect.*4.I come now to the third and laſt Stage of my undertaking, which is, to ſhew that Secret or Auricular Confeſſion, as it is now preſcribed and practiſed in and by the Church of *Rome*, is not only unneceſſary, and burdenſom in it ſelf, but alſo very miſchievous to Piety, and the great ends of Chriſtian Religion:

For the former part of this charge, if it be not evi- dent enough already, it will eaſily be made out from
the

the Premiſes, for they cannot deny that they make this kind of Confeſſion neceſſary to Salvation, at leaſt as neceſſary as Baptiſm it ſelf is, (ſuppoſing a Man hath ſinned after Baptiſm) now if it be neither made ſo by Divine Inſtitution, nor acknowledged to be ſo by the conſtant Opinion of the Church, what an horrible impoſition is here upon the Conſciences of Men, when in the higheſt and worſt ſenſe that can be they teach *for Doctrines the Commandments of Men,* and make Salvation harder than God hath made it, and ſuſpend mens hopes upon other terms then he hath done ? If it was preſcribed by the preſent Church as a matter of Order and Diſcipline only, or of convenience and expediency, we ſhould never boggle at it upon this account, or diſpute the point with them ; or if it was only declared neceſſary *pro hic & nunc,* upon extraordinary emergency, by the peculiar condition of the Penitent, his weakneſs of judgment, the perplexity of his Conſcience, his horrible guilt or extream Agonies, we would not differ with them upon that neither ; but when it is made neceſſary univerſally, and declared the indiſpenſable duty of all men whatſoever who have ſinned after Baptiſm (when God hath required no ſuch thing, but declares himſelf ſatisfied with true contrition and hearty remorſe for what is paſt, and ſincere Reformation for the time to come; this I ſay is an intolerable Tyranny and uſurpation upon the Conſciences of Men. And that is not all neither, for beſides its burdenſomneſs in the general, it particularly aggravates and increaſes a Mans other burdens, for inſtead of relieving perplexed Conſciences, which is the true and principal uſe of Confeſſions to Men, this prieſtly Confeſſion as it is preſcribed by the Council, intangles and afflicts them more ; for that injoyns that the Penitent lay open all his ſins, even the moſt ſecret, although

but.

but in thought or desire only, such as against the Ninth or Tenth Commandment, (according to their Division of the Decalogue,) now this is many times difficult enough ; but that's not all, he must also recount all the circumstances of these sins, which may increase or diminish the guilt, especially such as *alter the species and kind* of sin : Now what sad work is here for a Melancholy Man ? All the circumstances are innumerable, and how can he tell which are they that change the Species of the act, unless he be as great a Schoolman as his Confessor. Besides all this, it may be he is not very skilful in the distinction between venial and mortal sins, and if he omit one mortal sin, he is undone; therefore it is necessary for him (by consequence) to confess all venial sins too, and then where shall the poor Man begin, or when shall he make an end? Such a *Carnificina* such a rack and torture, in a word, such an Holy Inquisition is this business of Auricular Confession become. And that Eminent Divine of *Strasburgh* (of whom *Beatus Rhenanius* speaks) seems very well to have understood both himself, and this matter who pronounces that *Scotus* and *Thomas* had with their tricks, and subtilties, so perplexed this plain Business of Confession, that now it was become plainly impossible. And so much for that.

But as for the second part of this impeachment, *viz.* That the Auricular Confession now used in the Church of *Rome*, is mischievous to Piety ; This remains yet to be demonstrated, and we will do it the rather in this place, because it will be an abundant Confirmation of all that which hath been discoursed under the two former Heads; and might indeed have saved the labour of them, but that we were unwilling to leave any pretence of theirs undiscussed; for if this practice of theirs appear to be mischievous to Piety, it will

never

never by any ſober man be thought either to have
been inſtituted by our Saviour, or to have been the
ſenſe and uſage of the Catholick Church, whatever
they pretend on its behalf.

Now therefore this laſt and important part of my
charge I make good by theſe Three Articles following.

Firſt, This Method of theirs is dangerous to Piety,
as it is very apt to cheat People into an Opinion that
they are in a better Condition then truly they are,
or may be in towards God, as that their ſins are pardoned, and diſcharged by him, when there is no ſuch
matter. The Church-men of *Rome* complain of the
Doctrine of ſome reformed Divines touching aſſurance
of Salvation, that it fills men with too great confidence, and renders them careleſs and preſumptuous ;
but whatſoever there is in that, it is not my buſineſs
now to diſpute it, however methinks it will not very
well become a *Romaniſt* to aggravate it, till he have
acquitted himſelf in the point before us ; for by this
Aſſurance Office of theirs they comply too much with
the ſelf flattery of Mens own Hearts, they render Men
ſecure, before they are ſafe, and furniſh them with a
confidence like that of the Whore *Solomon* ſpeaks of,
who wipes her Mouth, and ſaith I have done no evil.
For Men return from the Confeſſors Chair (as they are
made to believe) as Pure as from the Font, and as In-
nocent as from their Mothers Womb ; as if God was
concluded by the act of the Prieſt, and as if he being
ſatisfied with an humble poſture, a dejected look,
and a lamentable murmur, God Almighty would be
put off ſo too.

Ah nimium faciles qui triſtia crimina, &c.

Ah cheating Prieſts who made fond Men believe,
That God Almighty pardons all you ſhrieve. Per-

Perhaps they will fay this is the fault and folly of the Men, not of the Inftitution of the Church : But why do they not teach them better then? Nay, why do they countenance and incourage them in fo dangerous miftakes? For whither elfe tend thofe words in the Decree of the Council of *Trent, ipfi Deo reconciliandis* ? *q. d.* that by this way of Confeffion, *&c.* men are reconciled to the Divine Majefty himfelf; or thofe other forecited, where the Prieft is faid to be the *Vicar of Chrift, and in his ftead,* a Judge or Prefident ; or efpecially what other meaning can thofe words have where it is faid, that *this Rite is as neceffary as Baptifm, for as in that all fins are remitted which were committed in former time, fo in this all fins committed after Baptifm are likewife remitted?*

Now I fay, what is the natural tendency of all this, but to make People believe that their Salvation or Damnation is in the Power of the Prieft, that he is a little God Almighty, and his difcharge would certainly pafs current in the Court of Heaven. But there is fophiftry and juggle in all this, as I thus make appear ; for,

1. The Prieft cannot pardon whom he will, let him be called *Judex* and *Præfes* never fo ; for if his Sentence be not according to Law it will be declared Null at the Great Day ; only it may be good and valid in the mean time *in foro Ecclefiæ* ; and here lies the cheat.

2. Nor are all fins retained or unforgiven with God, that are not pardoned by the Prieft ; it is true in publick Scandals, till the Sinner fubmit to the Church, God will not forgive him ; *For what that binds on Earth is in this fenfe bound in Heaven* ; but what hath the Church to do to retain, or to bind the Sinner in the cafe of fecret fins, where it can charge no guilt on him?

3. Nor

Seff. 14. Can. 1.

Ibid. Cap. 5.

Ibid. Cap. 2.

3. Nor is it properly the act of the **Prieſt** which pardons, but the Tenor of the Law, and the diſpoſition of Mind in the Penitent agreeable thereunto, qualifying him for Pardon, to which the Pardon is to be imputed : As it is not the Herald which pardons, but the Prince who by his Proclamation beſtows that Grace upon thoſe who are ſo and ſo qualified.

4. Nor, Laſtly, Can the Prieſt be ſaid to pardon ſo properly by thoſe Majeſtick words, *abſolvo te*, as by his whole Miniſtry, in inſtructing People in the Terms of the New Covenant, and making Application of that to them by the Sacraments ; this he hath Commiſſion to do, but thoſe big words I cannot find that he hath any where Authority to pronounce, and therefore (as I think I obſerved before) the Ancient Church had no form of Abſolution, but only receiving Penitents to the Communion : And the *Greek* Church had ſo much modeſty as to Abſolve in the third Perſon, not in the firſt, to ſhew that their Pardon was Miniſterial and Declarative only.

All theſe things notwithſtanding the People are let to go away with ſuch an Opinion as aforeſaid (becauſe it is for the Grandeur and Intereſt of the Prieſthood, that they ſhould be cheated; but theſe miſapprehenſions would vaniſh, if their teachers would be ſo juſt as to diſtinguiſh between God's Abſolution, and the Abſolution of the Church ; the firſt of which extends to the moſt ſecret ſins, the latter to open Scandals only ; the one delivers from all real guilt, the other from external Cenſure only ; of the latter the Prieſt may (by the leave of the Church) have the full diſpenſation, ſo that he is really pardoned with her that hath ſatisfied the Prieſt ; but of the former he diſpenſes but conditionally. To confirm all which I will here add only two Teſtimonies of the judgment of the AncientChurch.

G   The

The firſt is of *Firmilianus* Biſhop of *Cæſarea* in his Epiſtle to St. *Cyprian,* reckoned the Seventy Fifth of St. *Cyprians,* where ſpeaking of holding Eccleſiaſtical Councils every Year, he gives theſe reaſons for it; *Ut ſi qua graviora ſunt communi conſilio dirigantur, lapſis quoque fratribus,& poſt lavacrum ſalutare à Diabolo vulneratis, per pœnitentiam medela quæratur; non quaſi à nobis remiſſionem peccatorum conſequantur, ſed ut per nos ad intelligentiam delictorum ſuorum convertantur,& Domino plenius ſatisfacere cogantur;* partly (ſaith he) that by joint advice, and common conſent, we may agree upon an uniform Order in ſuch weighty Affairs as concern our reſpective Churches, partly that we may give relief, and apply a remedy to thoſe who by the temptation of the Devil have fallen into ſin after Baptiſm; *not that we can give them Pardon of their ſin, but that by our Miniſtry they may be brought to a knowledge of their ſins, and directed into a right courſe to obtain Pardon at the Hands of God.* The other is of *Theodorus* Arch-Biſhop of *Canterbury* whoſe words are theſe: *Confeſſio quæ ſoli Deo fit purgat peccata: Ea vero quæ Sacerdoti fit, docet qualiter purgentur. Confeſſion to God properly obtains the Pardon of Sin; but by Confeſſion to Men, we are only put into the right way to obtain pardon.* Thus they :

Theod. Cantuar.apudBeat. Rhen. *in præf. ad* Tertul. *de pœnit.*

But now in the Church of *Rome,* the caſe is otherwiſe ; there the Prieſt ſuſtains the Perſon of our Lord Jeſus Chriſt himſelf, and is not ſo much his Delegate as his Plenipotentiary, and his Pardon is as full and good as if the Judge of the World had pronounced it *pro Tribunali;* ſo that if the moſt lewd and habitual Sinner have but the good fortune to go out of the World under the Bleſſing of his Ghoſtly Father, that is to ſay, either death came ſo ſoon after his laſt Abſolution, or the Prieſt came ſo opportunely after his laſt ſin, that he

hath

hath not begun a new fcore, he is fure to go Heaven without more ado. This I reprefent as the firft mifchief attending their Doctrine, and Practice of Auricular Confeßion. But this is not all, for

Secondly, It corrupts and debauches the very Doctrine and Nature of Repentance which the whole Gofpel lays fo much ftrefs upon: Making Attrition (which is but a flight forrow for fin, or a diflike of it in Contemplation of the Wrath of God impendent over it) pafs for Contrition, which implies an hatred and deteftation of it for its own moral evil and deformity, with a firm refolution of amendment. This they many of them are not afhamed to teach, and their practice of Abfolution fuppofes and requires it. The Jefuites in particular, who have almoft ingroft to themfelves the whole Monopoly of Confeßions, avow this as their Principle. Father *Bauny*, *Efcobar*, and *Suarez* declare their Judgment, that the Prieft ought to abfolve a Man upon his faying, that he detefts his fin, although at the fame time the Confeffor doth not believe that he does fo. And *Cauffin* faith, if this be not true, there can be no ufe of Confeßions amongft the greateft part of Men. Thefe things (it's true) are difliked by fome others of the *Romanifts*, and the *Curees* of *France* are fo honeft as to cry fhame of it before all the World; for, fay they, Attrition is but the work of Nature, and if that alone will ferve for Pardon, then a Man may be pardoned without Grace. But therefore, fay the others, the Sacrament of Penance doth it alone, and this is for the Honour of the Sacrament; greatly for the Honour of it (fay I) that it is of greater power then our Lord Jefus Chrift, and his Gofpel, which cannot help a wicked Man to Heaven, whileft he continues fo, but this Sacrament it feems can. Nor can they excufe this matter by fay-

G 2   ing

ing thefe odious affertions are but the private Opinions of fome Divines. For they are plainly favoured by the determinations of the Council of *Trent* ; I confefs that Council delivers it felf warily and cunningly in this point (as it ufes to do in fuch cafes) yet thefe are their words, *Illa vero contritio imperfecta quæ attritio dicitur, quamvis fine Sacramento Pœnitentiæ per fe ad juftificationem perducere peccatorem nequeat, tamen eum ad Dei Gratiam in Sacramento Pœnitentiæ impetrandam difponit,* &c. Which is as much as to fay, though Attrition or a fuperficial Sorrow for Sin, barely, alone, and without Confeffion to a Prieft, will not juftify a Man before God, yet Attrition and Confeffion together will do it, for then they are as good as true Repentance. And in this fenfe *Melchior Canus* long fince thought he underftood the Council well enough.

Conc. Trident. Seff. 14. Cap 4.

Thirdly, This bufinefs of Auricular Confeffion, as it is practifed in the Church of *Rome,* is fo far from being a means to prevent and reftrain fin, as it highly pretends to be (and I am fure as it ought to be, if it be good for any thing) that contrariwife it is either loft labour, and a meer Ceremony, or it greatly incourages and imboldens, and hardens Men in it, both by the Secrecy, the Multitudes, and the Frequency of thefe Confeffions, by the curfory, hypocritical and evafive ways of confeffing, by the flight Penances impofed, and the cheapnefs, eafinefs, and even proftitution of Abfolutions.

It were eafy to be copious in inftances of all thefe kinds, but it is an uncomfortable fubject, and I haften to a conclufion; therefore I will only touch upon them briefly.

1. For the privacy of thefe Confeffions. In the Ancient Church (as I have noted before) the Scandalous Sinner was brought upon the Stage before a great Affembly

Aſſembly of Grave and Holy Men, he lay proſtrate on the ground, which he watered with his Tears, he crept on his Knees, and implored the Pitty and Prayers of all preſent, in whoſe countenances (if for ſhame he could look up) he ſaw abhorrence of his fact, indignation at God's diſhonour, conjoined with compaſſion to his Soul, and joy for his Repentance; his Confeſſion was full of remorſe and confuſion; the remedy was as ſharp and diſguſtful to Fleſh and Blood as the Diſeaſe had been pleaſant, and the pain of this expiation was able to imbitter the ſweet of Sin to him ever after. Or if the Confeſſion was not made before the whole Church, but to the Penitentiary only, yet he was a Grave and Holy Perſon, choſen by the Church, and repreſenting it, a Perſon reſident in that Church, and ſo able to take notice of, and mind the future Converſation of thoſe that addreſſed themſelves to him; a Perſon of that Sanctity and Reverence that he could not chooſe but deteſt and abhor all baſe and vile actions that ſhould come to his knowledge: Now it muſt needs be a terrible cut to a Sinner to have all his lewdneſs laid open before ſuch an one, and then to be juſtly, and ſharply rebuked by him, to have his ſins aggravated, and to be made to ſee his own ugly ſhape in a true glaſs held by him, beſides to be enjoined the performance of a ſtrict Penance of Faſting and Prayer, and after all (if this do not do) to have the Church made acquainted with the whole matter (as in the caſe of the Deacon aforeſaid.) This courſe was likely to work ſomething of remorſe in the Sinner for what was paſt, and to make him watchful and careful for the time to come.

But what is the way of the Church of *Rome* like to this? Where a Man may confeſs to any Prieſt, to him that knows him not, and ſo cannot obſerve his future

life

life and carriage; nay, perhaps that knows not how
to value the guilt of ſin, or to judge which be Venial,
and which Mortal Sins, or eſpecially what circumſtances do alter the ſpecies of it, and it may be too,
he may be ſuch an one that makes no Conſcience himſelf of the ſins I confeſs to him. Now, when all is tranſ-
acted between me and ſuch a Prieſt in a corner, and
that under the inviolable Seal of Confeſſion, what
great ſhame can this put me to? What remorſe is it
likely to work in me? What ſhall diſcourage me from
going on to *ſin again, if no worſe thing happen to
me?*

2. And then for the multitude of Confeſſions in the
Church of *Rome*, that alſo takes off the ſhame, and
weakens the efficacy of it, ſo that if it do no harm,
it is not likely to do any good; for who is concern'd much in the doing that which he ſees
all the World do as well as himſelf; if only notorious Sinners were brought to Confeſſion (as it
was in the Primitive Church) then it might pro-
bably and reaſonably provoke a bluſh, and cauſe a remorſe in him to whom ſuch a remedy was preſcribed;
but when he ſees the whole Pariſh, and the Prieſt too
brought to it, and Men as generally complying with
it, as they approach to the Lord's Table; What
great wonders can this work? What ſhame can it
inflict upon any Man! What effect can be expected from it, but that it ordinarily makes
Men ſecure and careleſs, and grow as familiar with
ſin as with the remedy, or at leaſt think as well of
themſelves as of other Men, ſince it ſeems they have as
much need of Confeſſion and abſolution as himſelf?

3. To which the frequency and often repetitions of
theſe kind of Confeſſions adds very much; it is very
likely ·

likely that modeſtly may work much upon a Man the
firſt or ſecond time he goes to Confeſſion, and it may
ſomething diſcompoſe his Countenance when he lays
open all his ſecret miſcarriages, to a Perſon eſpecially
for whom he hath a Reverence (for we ſee every
thing, even ſin it ſelf is modeſt in its beginnings;) and
no doubt it is ſome reſtraint of ſin whilſt a Man is
ſenſible that he muſt undergo a great deal of pain and
ſhame in vomiting up again his ſweet Morſels
which he eats in ſecret: But by that time he hath
been uſed to this a while, it grows eaſie and habitual
to him, and cuſtom hath made the very puniſhment pleaſant as well as the ſin; eſpecially, if we
add,

4. The formal, curſory, hypocritical, and illuſive
ways of Confeſſion in frequent uſe amongſt them; as
that a Man may chooſe his own Prieſt, and then to be
ſure the greateſt Sinner will have a Confeſſour right
for his turn, that ſhall not be too ſevere and ſcrupu-
lous with him; that a Man may confeſs *in tranſitu,* in
a hurry or huddle, and then there can be no remark
made upon his Perſon nor his ſins; that a Man may
make one part of his Confeſſion to one Prieſt, and re-
ſerve the other part for another, ſo that neither of
them ſhall be able to make any thing of it; that he
may have one Confeſſour for his Mortal ſins, and
another for his Venial; ſo that one ſhall ſave him, if
the other damn him; nay, for failing, the forgetful
ſinner may have another Man to confeſs for him, or
at leaſt he may confeſs, that he hath not confeſſed;
theſe and abundance more ſuch illuſive Methods are
in daily uſe amongſt them, and not only taken up by
the licentious and unconſcionable People, but allowed
by ſome or other of their great Caſuiſts; now let any
Man judge whether this be a likelier way to reſtrain ſin,

or

or to encourage it ; whether the eafinefs of the remedy (if this be one) muſt not of neceffity make the
Diſeaſe ſeem not very formidable ; in a word, whether
this be not a ridiculing their own Religion, and, which
is worſe, a teaching Men to be ſo fool hardy *as to make
a mock of fin.*

5. This ſad reckoning will be inflamed yet higher
if we conſider the ſlight Penances uſually impoſed by
theſe Spiritual Judges upon the greateſt Crimes. The
Council determines that the Confeſſour muſt be exactly
made acquainted with all the circumſtances of the ſin,
that ſo he may be able to adjuſt a Penance to it ; now
when ſome great ſin is confeſſed and that in very foul
circumſtances, if the Penance proportioned to it, by
the Prieſt be to ſay two or three *Pater Noſters,* or
Ave-Maria's extraordinary, to give a little Money in
Alms to the Poor or ſome Pious uſe, to kneel on his
bare knees before ſuch a Shrine, to kiſs ſuch an Image,
to go on Pilgrimage a few Miles to ſuch a Saint, or
at moſt to wear an Hair Shirt, or it may be to faſt
with Fiſh, and Wine, and Sweetmeats, &c. doth not this
make that ſin which is thus mawled and ſtigmatized,
look very dreadfully, can any Man find in his Heart
to ſin again, when it hath coſt him ſo dear already ?

Oh, but they will tell us theſe Penances are not intended to correſpond with the guilt of the ſin, but only to ſatisfy the debt of Temporal puniſhment. But
we had thought that the end of Penance had been, to
work in the Penitent a diſpoſition for Pardon, by giving him both opportunities and direction to expreſs
the ſincerity of his Repentance ; and this was the uſe
of Penance in the Primitive Church, together with
the taking off the Scandal from the Society ; and for
that other end how doth the Church of *Rome* know

ſo

ſo certainly that there is a debt of Temporal puniſhment remaining due, after the ſin is pardoned before
God; it is true, God may pardon ſo far only as he
pleaſes, he may reſolve to puniſh temporally thoſe
whom he hath forgiven eternally, as we ſee he did in
the caſe of *David;* but that this is not his conſtant
Method appears by this that our *Saviour* releaſes
the Temporal puniſhment to many in the Goſpel,
whoſe diſeaſes he cured, ſaying to them, *Your ſins
are forgiven you,* when as yet it did not appear that all
Scores were quitted with God ſo, but that they
might have periſhed eternally, if they did not prevent
it by Faith and Repentance.

6. But laſtly, to come to an end of this ſad ſtory,
the eaſineſs and proſtitution of their abſolutions in the
Church of *Rome* contributes, as much to the encoura-
ging of Vice and careleſneſs in Religion as any of the
former; for what elſe can be the natural effect and
conſequence of that ruled caſe among their Caſuiſts
(as I ſhew'd before) that the Prieſt is bound to abſolve him that confeſſes, and ſaith, he is ſorry for his
ſin, though he doth in his Heart believe that he is not
contrite, but that either the Prieſts Pardon is a very
cheat, or elſe that Pardon is due of courſe to the moſt
impenitent Sinner, and there is no more to do but *Confeſs and be Saved?* or what is the meaning of their
common practice to abſolve men upon their Death-
beds, whether they be contrite, or attrite, or neither,
at leaſt when they can give no Evidence of either? If
they intended this only for abſolution from the Cen-
ſures of the Church it might be called Charity, and
look ſomething like the practice of the Primitive
Church, which releaſed thoſe upon their Death-beds,
whom it would not diſcharge all their lives before, tho
not then neither without ſigns of Attrition and con-
H   trition

trition too ; but thefe pretend to quite another thing ; namely to releafe men *in fere Confcientiæ*, and to give them a Pafs-port to Heaven without Repentance, which is a very ftrange thing, to fay no worfe of it. Or to inftance one thing more, what is the meaning of their practice of giving Abfolution before the Penance is performed (as is ufual with them) unlefs this be it, that whether the Man make any Confcience at all how he lives hereafter, yet he is pardoned as much as the Prieft can do it for him, and is not this a likely way of reformation?

I conclude therefore now upon the whole matter that Auricular Confeffion, as it is ufed in the Church of *Rome*, is only an Artifice of greatening the Prieft, and pleafing the People; a trick of gratifying the undevout and impious as well as the Devout and Religious; the latter it impofes upon by its outward appearance of Humility and Piety; to the former it ferves for a palliative Cure of the Gripes of Confcience, which they are now and then troubled with; in reality it tends to make fin eafie and tolerable by the cheapnefs of its Pardon, and in a word, it is nothing but the Old Difcipline of the Church in Duft and Afhes. And therefore though the Church of *England* in her Liturgy, pioufly wifhes for the Reftauration of the Ancient Difcipline of the Church, it can be no defect in her that fhe troubles not her felf with this Rubbifh.

FINIS.   *A*

A POST-SCRIPT.

AFter I had finished the foregoing Papers, and most part of them had also past the Press, I happened to have notice that there was a Book just then come over from *France*, written by a Divine of the *Sorbone*, which with great appearance of Learning maintained the just contrary to what I had afferted (especially in the Hiftorical part of this Queftion) and pretended to prove from the moft Ancient Monuments of the Holy Scriptures, Fathers, Popes and Councils, that Auricular Confeffion had been the conftant Doctrine, and Univerfal and Uninterrupted ufage of the Chriftian Church for near 1300 years from the Times of our Saviour to the *Laterane* Council.

So foon as I heard this, I heartily wifhed, that either the faid Book had come out a little fooner, or at leaft that my Papers had been yet in my hands; to the intent that it might have been in my Power, to have corrected what might be amifs, or fupplied what was defective in that fhort Difcourfe, or indeed if occafion were, to have wholly fuppreft it.

For as foon as I entered upon the faid Book, and found from no lefs a Man than the Author himfelf, that he had diligently read over all that had been written on both fides of this controverfy, and that this work of his was the product of Eighteen years ftudy, and that in the prime of his years, and moft flouri-

thing

shing time of his parts, that it was published upon the maturest deliberation on his part, and with the greatest applause and approbation of the Faculty, I thought I had reason to suspect, whether a small Tract, written in haste by a Man of no Name, and full enough of other Business, could be fit to be seen on the same Day with so elaborate a work.

But by that time I had read a little further, I took Heart, and permitted the Press to go on ; and now, that I have gone over the whole, I do here profess sincerely, that in all that learned Discourse I scarcely found any thing which I had not foreseen, and as I think in some measure prevented. But certain I am, nothing occurred that staggered my Judgment, or which did not rather confirm me in what I had written ; for though I met with abundance of Citations, and a great deal of Wit, and Dexterity in the management of them, yet I found none of them come home to the point ; for whereas they sometimes recommend and press Confession of Sin in general sometimes to the Church, sometimes to the Priest or Bishop as well as to God Almighty : Again sometimes they speak great things of the Dignity of the Priest-hood, and the great Honour that Order hath in being wonderfully useful to the relief of Guilty or Afflicted Consciences, other while they treat of the Power of the Keys, and the Authority of the Church, the danger of her Censures, the Comfort of her Absolution, and the severity of her Discipline, &c. but all these things are acknowledged by us without laborious proof, as well as by our Adversaries : That which we demand, and expect therefore, is, where shall we find in any of the Ancient Fathers, Auricular Confession said to be a Sacrament, or any part of one ? Or where is the Universal necessity of it asserted ? Or that secret sins committed

mitted

mitted after Baptifm, are by no other means, or upon no other terms pardoned with God, then upon their being confeſſed to men ? In theſe things lies the hinge of our diſpute, and of theſe particulars one ought in Reaſon to expect the moſt direct and plain proof imaginable, if the matter was of ſuch Conſequence, of ſuch Univerſal practice and notoriety as they pretend; but nothing of all this appears in this Writer more than in thoſe that have gone before him. In contemplation of which I now adventure this little Tract into the World, with ſomewhat more of Confidence then I ſhould have done, had it not been for this occaſion.

But leſt I ſhould ſeem to be too partial in the Caſe, or to give too ſlight an account of this Learned Man's performance, the Reader who pleaſes ſhall be judge by a Specimen or two which I will here briefly repreſent to him.

The former of them ſhall be the very firſt argument or Teſtimony he produces for his Aſſertion, which I the rather make my choice to give inſtance in, becauſe no Man can be ſaid ingenuouſly to ſeek for faults, to pick and chooſe for matter of exception, that takes the firſt thing that comes to hand.

The buſineſs is this, Chap. 2. Page 11. of his Book he cites the Council of *Illiberis* (with a great deal of circumſtance) as the firſt Witneſs for his Cauſe, and the Teſtimony is taken from the Seventy Sixth Canon, the words are theſe, *Si quis Diaconum,* &c. *i. e.* If any Man ſhall ſuffer himſelf to be ordained Deacon, and ſhall afterwards be convicted to have formerly committed ſome Mortal (or Capital Crime ;) if the ſaid Crime come to light by his own voluntary Confeſſion, he ſhall for the ſpace of Three years be debarred the Holy Communion, but in caſe his ſin be diſcover-

ed.

ed and made known to the Church by some other hand, then he shall suffer Five years suspension, and after that be admitted only to Lay Communion.

Now who would have ever thought this passage fit to be made choice of as the first proof of Auricular Confession, or who can imagine it should be any proof at all, much less a clear or direct one?

Oh, but here is Confession! It may happen so if the party please, but it is not enjoyned, but voluntary, and that not Auricular neither, but unto the Church, at least for ought appears.

And it is confession of a secret Sin too! True it was so, till it was either confessed or betrayed.

And here is Penance imposed for a secret sin: True when it was become publick.

And here is a different degree of Penance imposed upon him that ingenuously confesses, from him that stays till he is accused, and hath his sin proved upon him : And good Reason, for the one gave tokens of Repentance, and the other none. But then here is ———— What? no Sacrament of Penance, no declared absolute necessity of Confession to Men in order to pardon with God, but only a necessity that when the Fact is become notorious, whether by the Confession of the Party, or otherwise, that the Church use her endeavours to bring the Sinner to Repentance, and free her self from Scandal by making a difference betwixt the Good and the Bad, the more hopeful, and the less.

If this be a clear and proper Argument for the necessity of Auricular Confession : God help poor *Protestants* that cannot discern it ; but oh the Wit of Man, and the Power of Learning and Logick! What may not such Men prove if they have a mind to it ?

The other passage I instance in, is in his Tenth Chapter, Pag. 156. *viz.* the Critical and Famous Business

of

of the *Nectarian* Reformation at *Conſtantinople*, of
which I have ſpoken ſomewhat largely in the foregoing Papers. Now for this: This Learned Gentleman
after he hath acknowledged very frankly that publick Confeſſion of ſins was the Ancient uſe of the
Church in the times of St. *Irenæus*, *Tertullian*, *Cyprian*, and *Origen*; that is, for the ſpace of about
Three hundred years, and that inſtead of that ancient
uſage (upon occaſion of the *Decian* Perſecution) a public
Penitentiary was appointed at *Conſtantinople*, and
moſt other Orthodox Churches, and in ſhort, after he
had with more ingenuity then ſome others of his party,
owned the undoubted Truth of the Relations of *Socrates* and *Sozomen* touching this Affair, and made
ſome Obſervations thereupon not much to the advantage of his cauſe, he at length delivers that which
would be very much to his purpoſe, if it could be credible; namely, that upon the whole matter *Nectarius*
in aboliſhing the Penitentiary, neither aboliſhed publick nor private Confeſſions, but inſtead of obliging
Men to go to the Penitentiary left every Man bound
to reſort to his reſpective *Dioceſan*, and confeſs
his ſins to him; and ſo Auricular Confeſſion is after
this change every whit as neceſſary as it was before;
very true (ſay I) it is as neceſſary now as it was before, for it was only voluntary before, and ſo it may
be after. But if the intention of *Nectarius*, and the
effect of that alteration was only the change of the
Perſon, and every Man ſtill obliged to confeſs to ſome
body, how comes it to be ſaid in the ſtory that every
Man was left to his own Conſcience, doth that word
ſignify the Biſhop? then we have found out a right
Fanatic *Dioceſan*, for they will all readily confeſs to this
Biſhop, and believe his Abſolution as ſufficient as any
Romaniſt of them all doth: And yet it ſeems to be undeniably

deniably plain that *Socrates* after this Reformation. thought of no other Confeſſor but this, nor imagined Men now bound to make any other Confeſſion, but this (which if it was not Auricular was very ſecret) for otherwiſe how comes it to paſs that he expoſtulates the matter with *Eudæmon* who adviſed this change, and bewail'd the danger of this liberty which was hereby given men, if they were as ſtrictly bound ſtill to confeſs to their Biſhop as they were before to the Penitentiary ; therefore the Truth of the Buſineſs ſeems evidently to be this, that men were now at liberty to make their Confeſſions of ſecret Sins voluntarily, as they were no doubt before the Inſtitution of a Penitentiary. And now what hath this Learned Gentleman gotten by muſtering up this ſtory ; well however the Concluſion muſt be held, let the Premiſſes look to themſelves.

I could find in my Heart (now my hand is in) to proceed further and to obſerve ; what pitiful ſhifts he is put to, in his Thirteenth Chapter, to evade the Teſtimonies, brought by Monſieur *Daillè* out of St. *Chryſoſtom* againſt his *Hypotheſis.* And the rather becauſe (out of mere tediouſneſs of writing) I in the foregoing Papers omitted to ſpecify the moſt remarkable diſcourſes which that excellent Author hath upon this Subject. But the Authorities are ſo plain and unanſwerable, and the Evaſions of this Gentleman ſo forced and palpable, that I think it needleſs to go about to vindicate the one, or confute the other ; for in ſpight of Art this ſame Thirteenth Chapter (we ſpeak of) will afford no leſs than Thirteen Arguments. againſt the neceſſity of Auricular Confeſſion.

F I N I S.